Jack

Enjoy

Fred

MAG-NAN-I-MOUS MONKEY AND

Gerald Giraffe

by Fred G. Weiss

MINDSTIR MEDIA

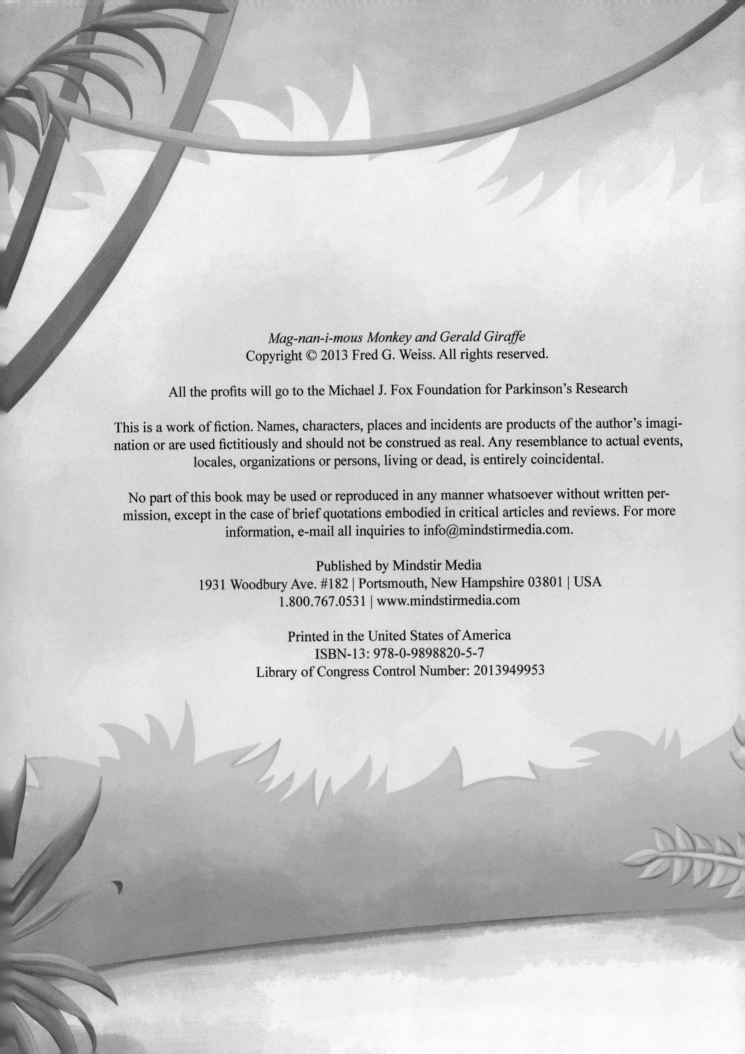

Published by Mindstir Media
1931 Woodbury Ave. #182 | Portsmouth, New Hampshire 03801 | USA
1.800.767.0531 | www.mindstirmedia.com

Printed in the United States of America
ISBN-13: 978-0-9898820-5-7
Library of Congress Control Number: 2013949953

Once upon a time, a very short while ago, a family of giraffes lived in the middle of the jungle in Africa. The youngest giraffe was Gerald. He was very young. He had never been away from his family.

On a bright clear morning, Gerald decided to go for a walk by himself. His family was busy bathing and drinking from the river. Gerald walked for a while. He stopped at the edge of the jungle. He used his long neck and sharp eyes to look out for lions and other dangerous animals, just the way his Mom and Dad did.

As Gerald was standing there, he felt a tap on his front leg.

TAP. TAP. TAP.

He looked down and he saw a monkey and he said, "Hello. Can I help you?"

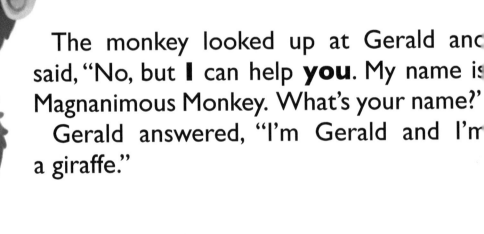

The monkey looked up at Gerald and said, "No, but **I** can help **you**. My name is Magnanimous Monkey. What's your name?"

Gerald answered, "I'm Gerald and I'm a giraffe."

Magnanimous Monkey said, "You know, with your yellow neck and brown spots, you stick out in the jungle. I think you need some camouflage."

Gerald said, "What's camouflage?"

"Camouflage makes you look like your surroundings, so you'll be safe from all the lions and dangerous animals," replied Magnanimous Monkey.

Gerald, being very young said, "That sounds like a good idea. What do I have to do?" Magnanimous Monkey said, "I'll take care of it," and off he ran. Magnanimous Monkey quickly came back with cans of paint. He painted Gerald from the top of his head down to the tip of his toes.

When he was done Magnanimous Monkey stood back and looked
"This is perfect camouflage," he told Gerald. "You look just like a
tree. You fit in with all the other trees."

No sooner had the paint dried when Gerald felt an awful pain on his neck. He heard a

PECK, PECK, PECK.

He shook his head and neck. Gerald looked down and saw a woodpecker jump off his neck.

The woodpecker looked up at him indignantly and said, "What are you doing? You're supposed to be a tree. I feed on trees. I'm supposed to be able to peck you!"

"But I'm **NOT** a tree. I'm a giraffe!" said Gerald.

"If you are a Giraffe then it's silly to see you look this way," said the woodpecker as he flew away in a huff.

Gerald was so distracted by the woodpecker that he failed to look for lions. All of a sudden, he heard the roar of a lion. Gerald was really scared. He turned and ran as fast as he could all the way back to his family.

When his Mother saw him, she said, "Gerald, you look ridiculous all painted that way. What happened?" Gerald told his Mom and Dad about Magnanimous Monkey.

Gerald's Mom looked at him and said, "Gerald, that was Magnanimous Monkey. He gives magnanimous advice to anyone silly enough to listen. Magnanimous advice is worth what you paid for it.

NOTHING!"

Gerald's Dad said, "Now you go in the river and wash yourself off. In the future use your long neck and sharp eyes to protect you from lions and other dangerous animals. That's what giraffes do."

CPSIA information can be obtained
at www.ICGtesting.com
Printed in the USA
LVIC01n1202051213
364019LV00017B/281